Without You

Without You

BY SARAH WEEKS · ILLUSTRATED BY SUZANNE DURANCEAU

LAURA GERINGER BOOKS *An Imprint of* HarperCollins*Publishers*

When the female emperor penguin lays her egg, she passes it straight to her mate, who puts it in a pouch just above his feet. Unlike most birds, she doesn't stay to help protect her young; instead, she goes out to sea to feed, leaving the male alone with the egg for two months in the freezing Antarctic winter.

During that time the temperature drops far below zero, and the penguins live in total darkness. The males, each with an egg balanced carefully on his feet, live off only their own stored body fat.

Huddled together for
warmth, the vigilant emperors
constantly move and shift on the ice so that
each bird gets his share of protected time in the
warmer inner circle as well as on the chilly
perimeter, serving as a wind barrier for others. Soon
after the eggs hatch, the females return to the
colony. In the darkness the only way for the
birds to recognize each other is by their
voices, so they call to their mates as
loudly as they can. When the pairs
have reunited, the fathers gently
transfer the precious chicks to
the mothers' feet and go off
to sea to feed.

She'll come back to you
And me soon,
You'll see....

No sun shining down on us.
It's black as pitch all day.

I feel a little funny inside.
My mamma's far away.

Nothin' but sea ice for miles around.
You close your eyes to the blinding sleet.
But here I am warm as toast,
Balancing on your feet.

Where would I be,
What would I do,
Who in the world would see me through...
Where would I be,
What would I do,
Without you?

We huddle together in the inner circle.

We serve our time on the outside too.

Brave the blizzards and the sad times,

While Mamma dives in the deep sea blue.

Nothin' but sea ice for miles around.
You duck your head when the cold wind blows.
But here I sit safe and sound,
Balancing on your toes.

Where would I be,
What would I do,
Who in the world would see me through...
Where would I be,
What would I do,
Without you?

I know that she's somewhere out there
Without us.

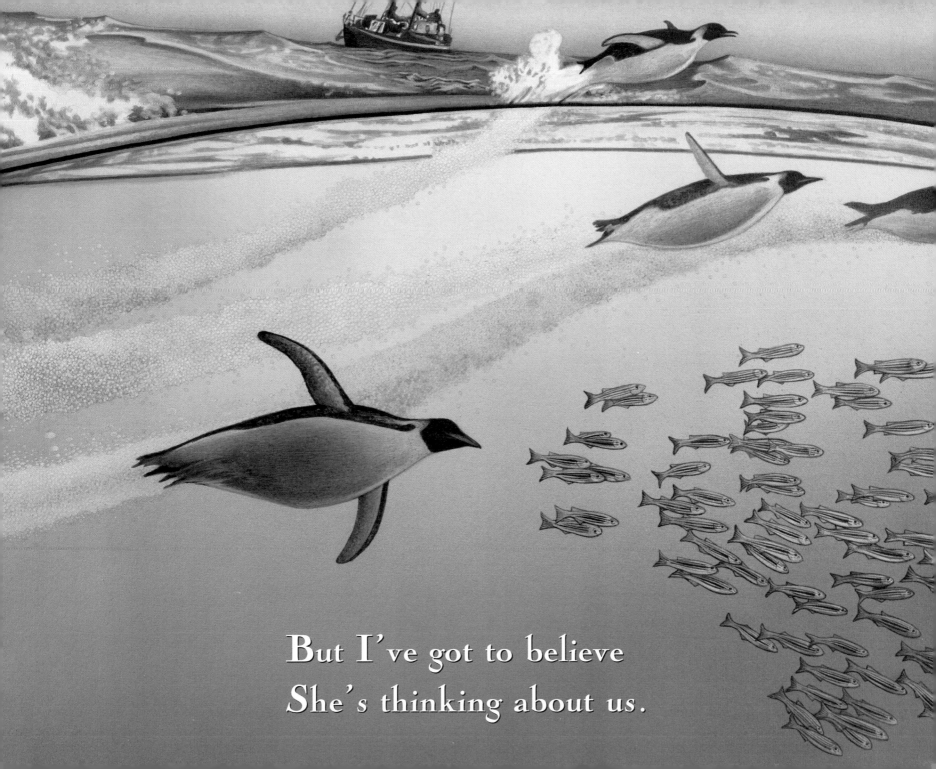

But I've got to believe
She's thinking about us.

She'll come back to you
And me soon,
You'll see....

No matter what,
You've got to stay awake now.
Don't let your eyes close.
When Mamma calls, you've got to answer for me.
Yours is the only voice she knows.

Where would I be,
What would I do,
Who in the world would see me through…
Where would I be,
What would I do…

Without you?

In loving memory of my
father, Robert Weeks.
—S.W.

This book is for you, Dad.
—S.D.

The illustrator would like to acknowledge Frans Lanting for the use
of some of his photographs as art references, courtesy of Minden Pictures.

Without You
Text copyright © 2003 by Sarah Weeks   Illustrations copyright © 2003 by Suzanne Duranceau
Manufactured in China. All rights reserved. No part of this book may be used or reproduced in any manner
whatsoever without written permission except in the case of brief quotations embodied in critical articles and reviews.
For information address HarperCollins Children's Books, a division of HarperCollins Publishers,
1350 Avenue of the Americas, New York, NY 10019.
www.harpercollinschildrens.com
Library of Congress Cataloging-in-Publication Data
Weeks, Sarah.
Without you / by Sarah Weeks ; illustrated by Suzanne Duranceau.
p.   cm.
Summary: A young penguin and his father receive comfort from each other as they
wait for the mother penguin to return from her diving.
ISBN-10: 0-06-027816-1 (trade bdg.) — ISBN-13: 978-0-06-027816-8 (trade bdg.)
ISBN-10: 0-06-000733-8 (lib. bdg.) — ISBN-13: 978-0-06-000733-1 (lib. bdg.)
ISBN-10: 0-06-113998-X (pbk.) — ISBN-13: 978-0-06-113998-7 (pbk.)
1. Penguins—Juvenile fiction. [1. Penguins—Fiction. 2. Parent and child—
Fiction.] I. Duranceau, Suzanne, ill. II. Title.
PZ10.3.W4215Wi 2003 [E]—dc21 99-34232 CIP AC
Typography by Alicia Mikles
❖ First Edition